Richard Scarry's
FUNNIEST STORYBOOK EVER!

This 2016 edition was published in the United States by Golden Books, an imprint of Random House
Children's Books, a division of Penguin Random House LLC, 1745 Broadway, New York, NY 10019,
and in Canada by Random House of Canada, a division of Penguin Random House Ltd, Toronto.
Originally published in a slightly different form by Golden Books, New York, in 1972.
Golden Books, A Golden Book, A Big Golden Book, the G colophon, and the distinctive gold spine are
registered trademarks of Penguin Random House LLC.
Visit us on the Web! randomhousekids.com
Educators and librarians, for a variety of teaching tools, visit us at RHTeachersLibrarians.com
Library of Congress Control Number: 2015935885
ISBN 978-0-385-38297-7
MANUFACTURED IN MALAYSIA
10 9 8 7 6 5 4 3 2
Random House Children's Books supports the First Amendment and celebrates the right to read.

Absent-Minded Mr. Rabbit

Mr. Rabbit walked down the street.
He wasn't looking at the workmen,
who were making a new, hot, sticky, gooey street.
No! He was looking at his newspaper.

He wasn't looking at his feet,
which were getting hot and sticky and gooey, too.
No! He was looking at his newspaper.

Then suddenly he stopped looking at his newspaper.
He looked down at his feet instead.
And do you know what he saw?
He saw that he was STUCK in that
hot, sticky, gooey street!

The workmen got a long pole and tried
to poke him out. It didn't work.

A truck tried to pull him out with a rope.
No good! He was stuck, all right!

They tried to blow him out with a huge fan.
The fan blew off his hat and coat . . .
but Mr. Rabbit remained stuck.

Some firemen tried to squirt him out.
They squirted water at his shirt and necktie—
but Mr. Rabbit remained stuck. REALLY STUCK!

Well, now! He can't stay there forever!
Somebody has to think of a way to get him out.

Aha! Here comes a power shovel!
Let's see what it will try to do.

Well, the power shovel reached down . . .
and scooped up Mr. Rabbit.

It dropped him gently to the dry ground.
He would certainly have to wash his feet when he
got home, but at least he was no longer stuck.
  He put on his clothes and thanked everyone.
As he was leaving, he promised that after this
he would always look where he was going.

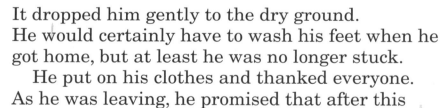

But a little while later he was reading his newspaper again. He had forgotten his promise. And, naturally, he wasn't watching where he was going.

OH!!! DON'T LOOK!!!!

Sergeant Murphy and the Banana Thief

Sergeant Murphy was busy putting parking tickets
on cars when, suddenly, who should come running
out of the market but Bananas Gorilla.
He had stolen a bunch of bananas, and was trying
to escape.

Murphy! LOOK! He is stealing your motorcycle, too!

Sergeant Murphy was furious.
Huckle and Lowly Worm were watching.
Huckle said, "You may borrow my tricycle
to chase after him if you want to."

B-r-e-e-e-t!

Away they went . . . chasing
after that naughty thief.

They raced through the crowded streets.
Don't YOU ever ride your tricycle in the street!

They crossed a drawbridge just as it
was opening to let a boat go through.

11

Bananas stopped suddenly and went into a restaurant.

Murphy said to Louie, who was the owner,
"I am looking for a thief!"
Together, they searched the whole restaurant,
but they couldn't find Bananas anywhere.

Louie then said, "Sit down and relax, Murphy.
I will bring you and your friends something delicious to eat."

Somebody had better pick up those banana peels
before someone slips on one. Don't you think so?

Louie brought them a bowl of banana soup. Lowly said, "I'll bet Bananas Gorilla would like to be here right now."

"Huckle, we mustn't forget to wash our hands before eating," said Sergeant Murphy. So they walked back to the washroom. Lowly went along, too.

When they came back, they discovered that their table had disappeared.

Indeed, it was slowly creeping away . . . when it slipped on a banana peel! And guess who was hiding underneath.

Sergeant Murphy, we are very proud of you! Bananas must be punished. Someday he has to learn that it is naughty to steal things that belong to others.

13

Speedboat Spike

Speedboat Spike liked to take his little boy, Swifty, out for a ride in his speedboat. Oh, my! Didn't Spike think he was smart!

Once he rammed into a sailboat.

Say! Why don't you look where you're going?

Another time he bumped into a barge and knocked a lady's laundry overboard. (Swifty! Why don't you tell your father to stop being such a dangerous driver?)

Speedboat Spike just wouldn't slow down,
and he wouldn't stop bumping into things.

STOP!

But that was before Officer Barnacle caught him . . . and made him stop!

Officer Barnacle ordered Speedboat Spike to keep
his speedboat in a wading pool UP ON LAND!
Now Spike can go as fast as he likes,
but he won't be able to bump into anyone.

But who is that I see
in that tiny little speedboat?
Why, it's his little boy, Swifty!
Oh dear! I think we are going to need
another wading pool.
Go get him, Officer Barnacle!

15

Ma Pig's New Car

Pa Pig bought a new car to give
to Ma Pig on her birthday.
She will certainly be surprised
when she sees her new car, won't she?

On the way home, Pa stopped at a drugstore.
When he came out, he got into a jeep by mistake.
(You should be wearing glasses, Pa Pig!)
Harry and Sally thought that Pa had swapped cars with a soldier.

Stop, thief!

Then he went to the supermarket.
When he came out he got into a police car.
"You made a good swap, Daddy," said Harry.
But Pa wasn't listening . . . and he didn't seem to be
thinking very well either. Don't you agree?

16

Next he drove to a fruit stand to buy some apples.
When he left he took Farmer Fox's tractor.
My, but Pa is absent-minded, isn't he?
   "Ma will certainly like her new tractor,"
said Sally to Harry.

They stopped to watch a fire.
When the fire was out they left—
in the fire engine!
How can *anyone* make so many mistakes?

Then they stopped to watch some workers
who were digging a big hole in the ground.
No! Pa did NOT get into that dump truck.
   But by mistake, he got into . . .

Hey, Joe!
You forgot
to turn off
the motor.

. . . Roger Rhino's power shovel!
 Ma Pig was certainly surprised to see her new CAR!
But, Pa! Do you know how to stop it?

Yes, he did!

Oh, oh! Here comes Roger now.
He has found Ma Pig's new car
and is bringing it to her.
 It looks as though he is very angry
with that someone who took his power shovel.

ROGER! PLEASE BE CAREFUL! You are squeezing
Ma's little car just a little bit too tightly.
 Well, let's all hope that Pa Pig will never
again make *that* many mistakes in one day!

Mr. Fixit

Mr. Fixit can fix ANYTHING.
At least that is what he once told me.

He fixed the wheel on Philip's wagon.

He fixed Mrs. Pussycat's automobile.

He fixed Sam's boat so that
it wouldn't ever leak again.
My, that was a leaky boat!

19

He fixed the flat tire
on the school bus.
Don't you think that you
should stop now, Mr. Fixit?

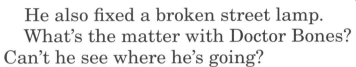

He also fixed a broken street lamp.
What's the matter with Doctor Bones?
Can't he see where he's going?

Dadda!

Mary's talking doll couldn't
say "Mamma" anymore.
Mr. Fixit fixed it.
Now it says "Dadda."

He fixed Mother Cat's vacuum
cleaner, but he made a little
mistake.
It won't vacuum the floor
anymore. Only the ceiling!
Mr. Fixit told her that she was
lucky to be the only one with
a vacuum cleaner like that!

He fixed Lowly Worm's shoe.
"You are a genius," said Lowly.
"I'll bet that there isn't anything
that you can't fix."
"You are right, Lowly," said
Mr. Fixit. "I can fix anything!"

Then Mr. Fixit went home for supper.
After his wife kissed him, she said,
"Will you please give Little Fixit
his bottle while I am fixing supper?"
Mr. Fixit filled the baby bottle
with milk. BUT . . . he didn't know
how to fix the nipple on the top.

He tried and he tried, but he couldn't
get it on. What a mess he was making!

Little Fixit said, "Daddy, let me try."
"It *can't* be done," said Mr. Fixit.
But he let Little Fixit try anyhow.
And Little Fixit fixed it—

on the very first try!

"WHY, THAT'S AMAZING!" said Mr. Fixit.
"Show *me* how to do it."
Now, just be patient, Mr. Fixit.
Let him finish his bottle first
and then he will show you how.

21

The Three Sitters

Mother Bear saw Wolfgang, Benny, and Harry
walking by. She ran out and said, "My house
is a mess. I've got to clean it from top
to bottom. Will you please baby-sit with Robert
while I go shopping for some soap?"

Wolfgang, Benny, and Harry all agreed to stay
and play with Robert while Mother Bear was shopping.

After a while they got tired of playing.
"I have a good idea," said Harry. "Let's make
some fudge."
(I don't think Mother Bear would approve of that,
do you?)

When they had finished mixing everything together, they poured it into a pan. (Do you suppose they *really* know how to make fudge?)

Then they all sat down at the kitchen table to wait for the fudge to cook.
Gurgle, burble! Burble, gurgle!
Something seems to be bubbling over!

POP!!!!
The oven door burst open.
The fudge had exploded!
RUN! RUN FOR YOUR LIVES!

23

Lowly ran to the telephone.
"HELP!" he cried. "The fudge is rising!
Our house is sinking in fudge!"

Look out, everyone! Here come the firemen now.
My, they are quick.

24

But, Lowly, WAIT!
Don't turn on the water hydrant
until the firemen attach the big hose to it.

Soon every bit of fudge had been washed
out of the house—along with a few other things.
But LOOK! Who is that coming?
Why, it's Mother Bear. Hurry up, fellows!
Straighten the house before she gets home.
Put everything back in place.
    And hurry up they did!

"I have never seen my house looking so spic
and span," said Mother Bear. "I think we should
have a party. Who would like to make some fudge?"
    Lowly spoke right up. "I think it would be
better if you made it, Mother Bear."
    And so she did. And everyone ate the best fudge
in the cleanest, spic-est, span-est house ever!

Tanglefoot

Tanglefoot was going to the supermarket to buy a can of soup for his mother. She told him to be careful not to trip or fall.

"I never trip or fall," said Tanglefoot.

1
one

He tripped and fell out the front door.

2
two

He tumbled over a baby carriage.

3
three

He then fell into the supermarket.

4
four

He bumped into the grocer.

5
five

He knocked over the butcher.

6

six

He tripped . . . and cans of soup went flying all over.

7

seven

O-O-O-F! Big Hilda was in his way.

"I must stop tripping and falling," he said to himself.

8

eight

But then he fell over the check-out counter.

He walked home without tripping once. Very good, Tanglefoot! He even helped his mother make a big bowl of soup for supper.

9

nine

But when she poured it into a big bowl, he fell into it!

Tanglefoot said, "I don't think I can trip and fall once more today."

10

ten

But he did!

Good night, Tanglefoot. Sleep tight.

27

The Talking Bread

Humperdink, the baker, was mixing bread dough with the help of Able Baker Charlie Mouse. His little girl, Flossie, watched them squish and squash the dough.

After they had kneaded the dough by squishing and squashing, they patted it into loaves of all different shapes and sizes.

Then Humperdink put the uncooked loaves of bread into the hot oven to bake.

After the loaves had finished baking,
Humperdink set them out on the table to cool.
M-m-m-m-m! Fresh bread smells good!

Mamma!

Finally he took out the last loaf.
LISTEN! Did you hear that?
When he picked up that loaf, it
said, "Mamma." But everybody knows
that bread can't talk.
IT MUST BE HAUNTED!!!

"HELP! POLICE!"
Humperdink picked up Flossie and ran from the
room.
"I must telephone Sergeant Murphy," he said.

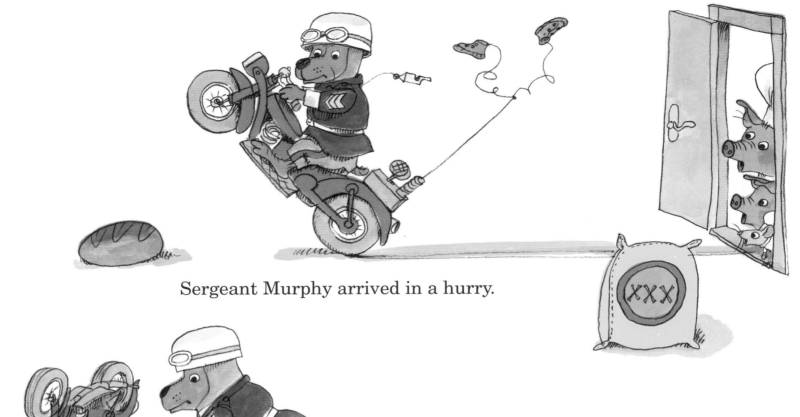

Sergeant Murphy arrived in a hurry.

He reached down and picked up
the loaf of haunted bread.

Mamma!

"Mamma!" the bread said.

Murphy was so startled he
fell into the mixing trough.

At just that moment, Huckle
and Lowly came into the bakery.

"That is a *very* strange loaf of bread," said Lowly.
Stretching out, he slowly ooched across the floor toward it.

He took a nibble.
The bread said nothing.

He nibbled and nibbled until only his foot was showing . . . and still the bread said nothing.

Mamma!

Lowly stood up.
The bread said, "Mamma!"

Lowly took another nibble, then stuck out his head.
"I have solved the mystery," he said. "Break the loaf open very gently, but *please* . . . don't break me!"

Mamma!

Baby!

Humperdink gently broke open the bread and inside was . . . Flossie's DOLL!
It had fallen into the mixing trough and had been baked inside the bread.

With the mystery solved, they all sat down to eat the haunted bread.
All of them, that is, except Lowly.
He had already eaten his fill.

All right, Lowly! Please take your foot off the table!

31

The Three Fishermen

Lowly, Huckle, and Daddy were going fishing.

Their little motorboat took them far away from shore.

Daddy said, "Throw out the anchor, Lowly."
Lowly threw the anchor out . . . and himself with it!

Lowly climbed back in and Daddy began to fish.

Daddy caught an old bicycle. But he didn't want an old bicycle. He wanted a fish.

Then Huckle fell overboard.
Wouldn't you know that something
like that would happen?

Daddy pulled Huckle out.
Why, look there! Huckle caught
a fish in his pants!

Daddy fished some more, but he
couldn't catch anything.
He was disgusted.
"Let's go home," he said. "There
just aren't any fish down there."

As Daddy was getting out of the boat,
he slipped . . . and fell!
Oh, boy! Is he ever mad now!

But why is he yelling so loudly?

33

Aha! I see!
A fish was biting his tail.
The fish was trying to catch Daddy.
It is good that Daddy has a strong tail.
Now Lowly is the only one who hasn't caught . . .

Wow!

But look! Lowly has taken off his hat.
Do you see what is under it?
A FISH! Very good, Lowly.

Yes, there you see three
very good fishermen!

The Accident

Harvey Pig was driving down the street.
(Better keep your eyes on the road, Harvey.)

Well! He didn't keep his eyes on the road
and he had an accident.

B-r-e-e-e-t!

Sergeant Murphy came riding along.
"Everyone get on the sidewalk," he said.
"I don't want anyone arguing in the street.
You might get run over."
So everyone got on the sidewalk.

35

And just in time, too!
Rocky was driving his bulldozer down the street.
"I'm very sorry about that," he said. "I guess
I wasn't looking where I was going."

All right, now. Keep calm, everybody!
Here comes Greasy George, the garage mechanic.

Greasy George towed away the cars, and the motorcycle, and all the loose pieces.
"I will fix everything just like new," he said. "Come and get them in about a week."

Greasy George worked and worked to make everything just like new again. Stand back, Lowly and Huckle! Don't get too close to him!

Well! Greasy George was certainly telling the truth. When everyone came back, everything was certainly NEW! I don't know how you did it, Greasy George, but I think you got the parts a little bit mixed up!

My cap!

Calling Sergeant Murphy!
Your little girl, Bridget,
won't take her nap.
Hurry home immediately.

Please Move to the Back of the Bus

Ollie was a bus driver.
All day long he called out
to his passengers, "Please
move to the back of the bus."

At every single bus stop, he would politely
say, "Please move to the back of the bus.
There are others who want to get on."

My, see how his bus is filling up!

But look there! The back of the bus is empty.
No one will move back. Ah! Here comes Big Hilda.
She will move to the back of the bus.

Big Hilda just managed to squeeze on.
By this time Ollie was furious.
"I am not going to drive any farther,"
he shouted, "until everyone moves to the back
of the bus!"

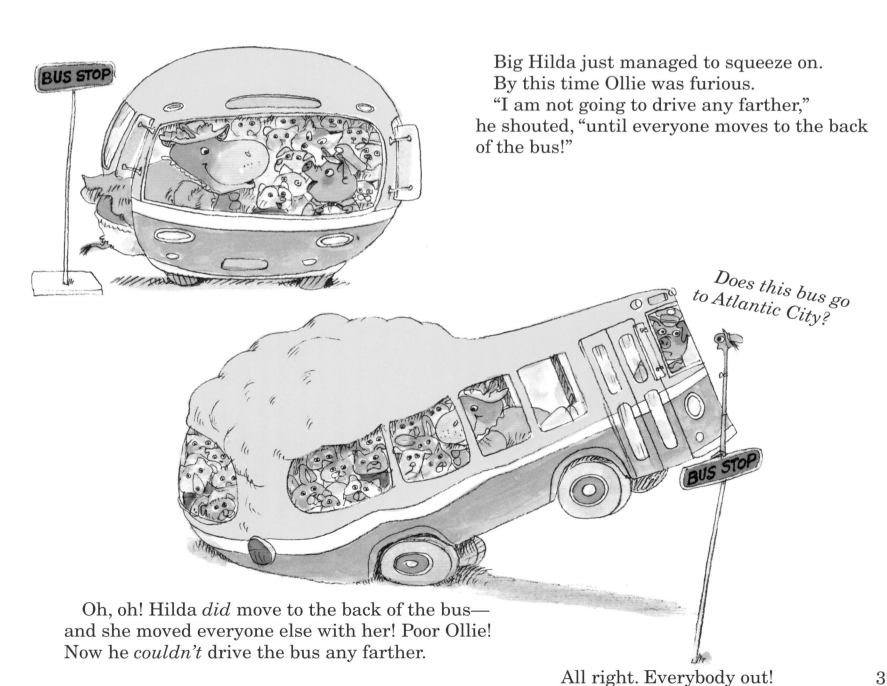

*Does this bus go
to Atlantic City?*

Oh, oh! Hilda *did* move to the back of the bus—
and she moved everyone else with her! Poor Ollie!
Now he *couldn't* drive the bus any farther.

All right. Everybody out!
This is the end of the line.

39

Uncle Willie and the Pirates

Not a soul dared to go sailing.
Do you know why?
   There was a wicked band
of pirates about, and they would
steal anything they could get
their hands on!
   But Uncle Willy wasn't afraid.
"They won't bother me," he said.

He dropped his anchor near a deserted island.
Aunty Pastry had baked him a pie for his lunch.
"I think I will have a little nap before I
eat my pie," said Uncle Willy to himself.

Uncle Willy went to sleep. *B-z-z-z-z-z.*
What is THAT I see climbing on board?
A PIRATE! And another! And another?
PIRATES, UNCLE WILLY!

40

But Uncle Willy couldn't do a thing.
There were just too many pirates.

First, they put Uncle Willy on the deserted
island. Then they started to eat his pie.
"M-m-m-m-m! DEE-licious!" they all said.

Uncle Willy was furious. He didn't care
so much about the pie, but he needed his boat
if he was ever going to get home again.

Then Uncle Willy had an idea.
He gathered some branches, some sea shells,
and some long beach grass. He wove the
beach grass into a kind of cloth.

41

Then he tied some sea shells onto the branches and made a ferocious-looking mouth.

He tied the grass cloth onto the mouth, then attached some sea-shell eyes. By the time he tied on a spiky palm leaf, he had made a ferocious MONSTER!

Uncle Willy got inside. He was now "Uncle Willy, THE FEROCIOUS MONSTER." Look out, you pirates!

The Ferocious Monster swam out to the boat. The pirates were terrified.

They all ran into the cabin to hide.
The Ferocious Monster closed the door
behind them—and locked it.

   The Monster had captured
the wicked pirates!

   Then the Monster sailed back home.
Aunty Pastry saw it from the dock.
She was terrified!
   "There is a horrible Monster coming!"
she cried. "He is even worse than the pirates!"

   Uncle Willy landed, and took off his monster suit.
   Everyone said, "Thank goodness it was only you!"
   Sergeant Murphy took the pirates away to be punished.

   Well . . . Uncle Willy had made
the seas safe to sail on again.
Hurray for Uncle Willy—
   THE FEROCIOUS MONSTER!!!

How was the pie, Uncle Willy?

You BAD pie rats!!!

The Unlucky Day

Mr. Raccoon opened his eyes.
"Wake up, Mamma," he said.
"It looks like a good day."

He turned on the water.
The faucet broke off.
"Call Mr. Fixit, Mamma," he said.

He sat down to breakfast.
He burned his toast.
Mamma burned his bacon.

Mamma told him to bring
home food for supper.
As he was leaving, the
door fell off its hinges.

Driving down the road,
Mr. Raccoon had a flat tire.

While he was fixing it,
his pants ripped.

44

He started again.
His car motor exploded
and wouldn't go any farther.

He decided to walk.
The wind blew his hat away.
Bye-bye, hat!

While chasing after his hat,
he fell into a manhole.

The he climbed out and
bumped into a lamp post.

A policeman yelled at him
for bending the lamp post.

"I must be more careful,"
thought Mr. Raccoon. "This is
turning into a bad day."

He didn't look where he was
going. He bumped into Mrs. Rabbit
and broke all her eggs.

Another policeman gave him
a ticket for littering the
sidewalk.

His friend Warty Wart Hog came up
behind him and patted him on the back.
Warty! Don't pat so hard!

"Come," said Warty. "Let's go
to a restaurant for lunch."

45

Warty ate and ate and ate.
Have you ever seen such bad
table manners?
Take off your hat, Warty!

Warty finished and left without
paying for what he had eaten.
Mr. Raccoon had to pay for it.
Just look at all the plates
that Warty used!

The lunch cost Mr. Raccoon
every penny he had with him.
"What other bad things can
happen to me today?" he wondered.

Well . . . for one thing, the tablecloth could catch on his belt buckle!

46

"Don't you ever come in here again!" the waiter shouted.

"I think I had better get home as quickly as possible," thought Mr. Raccoon. "I don't want to get into any more trouble."

He arrived home just as Mr. Fixit was leaving.
Mr. Fixit had spent the entire day finding new leaks.
"I will come back tomorrow to fix the leaks," said Mr. Fixit.

Mrs. Raccoon asked her husband if he had brought home the food she asked for. She wanted to cook something hot for supper. Of course Mr. Raccoon hadn't, so they had to eat cold pickles for supper.

After supper they went upstairs to bed.
"There isn't another unlucky thing that can happen to me today," said Mr. Raccoon as he got into bed. Oh, dear! His bed broke! I do hope that Mr. Raccoon will have a better day tomorrow, don't you?

Rudolf's Airplane

Happy landing!

LOOK OUT, EVERYONE!
Rudolf von Strudel has fallen
out of his airplane, and the plane
might crash on top of you!

49

Oh! *That* was a *great* place
for his plane to land. Wasn't it?
But how will they ever get it down?
The fire ladder is not long enough,
and I don't think *anyone* will
be able to climb up *that* high.
But there has to be *some* way!

Well, Rudolf, at least, has landed safely.

Lowly and Huckle saw it all happen.
And Lowly had an idea for getting the plane down.
He told Huckle about it.

"That's a good idea, Lowly," said Huckle.
"Let's do it."

First, Huckle broke a branch
off a tree. Then, with a piece
of string, he made a bow.
He was going to shoot
an arrow into the air.
But where would he get the arrow?

Lowly was going to be the arrow!

AOK!

Huckle shot Lowly into the air.
Up, up, up he went . . .

. . . and landed in the cockpit
of Rudolf's plane.
Lowly started the motor,
and the plane took off.

Does Lowly know how to *fly*?
Of course Lowly knows how to fly.
But does Lowly know how to *land*?
Of course Lowly knows how to land!

Well! I suppose that's
ONE way to land an airplane!
Very good, Lowly!

*I think
I need
more
practice.*

Lowly Worm's Birthday

It was Lowly's birthday. Mother Cat was going to bake a birthday cake. Father was going to town to buy some eggs for the cake, and some candles to put on it. And maybe a few other things as well.

"Be careful you don't break the eggs," said Mother.

Father Cat stopped at the hardware store to buy some birthday candles. HE LEFT THE CAR MOTOR RUNNING!!! You know better than to do THAT, Father Cat.

Now! See what happened.
The car drove off all by itself!
I don't think Lowly knows how to drive.
Anyway, he certainly doesn't have a driver's license.

JOE'S HARDWARE STORE

BIRTHDAY CANDLES ON SALE HERE

The car headed for the supermarket
to get the eggs for Lowly's birthday cake.
As it went past the egg counter,
Lowly picked up some fresh eggs.
Father Cat had to pay the cashier for them.

pickles

SPECIAL TODAY! FRESH EGGS IN A BASKET

MAKE ALL DELIVERIES AT THIS DOOR

CAFÉ OLÉ

GAR AND BA
SANITATI
ENGINEE

They drove out
through the back door
of the supermarket.

MADAME OVERALL'S
PARTY SHOP
BOOKS • FAVORS

BOOKS

CREAM

They passed Mr. Fixit, who was
fixing a broken traffic light.
Hurry up and fix it, Mr. Fixit,
before there is a bad accident!

Don't be a
litterbug!

Hang on to those eggs, Lowly
. . . and don't break any!

But where is Father Cat?
Oh! There he is! He has just bought some
balloons and favors at the party shop.

57

Through Farmer Alfalfa's hayfield they went.
I don't think Farmer Alfalfa liked that.
But then . . . it was the car's fault.
No one was steering it.

Father Cat was still chasing after them.
He stopped for a moment in order to buy
some of Mrs. Alfalfa's delicious fresh strawberries.
He thought they would look very nice
on Lowly's birthday cake.

At last they all came to a stop in Mother Cat's kitchen!

My babies! My Lowly!